CW00850671

Hanauma Bay

Within minutes of receiving their orders, top-ranked agents, Megan and Marcus Morgan, who work for the secret organisation known as EP, are embarking on their second thrilling mission to solve an environment-related beach mystery. Their incredible beach hut, Parry, magically transports them from their holiday at Bexhill-On-Sea in East Sussex to the faraway tropical paradise of Hanauma Bay in Hawaii. Setting to work quickly, Megan and Marcus soon discover that rubbish is mysteriously mounting in the bay, threatening to destroy the reef and marine life within days. When the dangerous investigation starts to go wrong, the children find themselves held as captives by ruthless criminals in a camouflaged rubbish dump. It seems that Megan and Marcus are destined for destruction – but can they escape and save Hanauma Bay – or will this beautiful beach paradise be gone forever?

Secret agents everywhere are invited to step inside the amazing Bexhill-On-Sea beach hut of The Paradise Beach Mysteries and join Marcus and Megan Morgan, as they travel at the speed of light to far-away top-rated world beaches, in a quest to save them from environmental ruin.

Hanauma Bay

The Paradise Beach Mysteries

Cathy Maisano

ISBN 978-1512253115

Edited by Rosemary Bickle
www.writeforchildren.co.uk

Illustrations by Claire Fletcher
Copyright © 2015

For Gabriel and Francesca

Contents

Chapter One

'Where on earth did you find that?' Megan gasped. She had never seen a diamond ring so big, round and shining. It belonged on the finger of a movie star – not in the small, wet and sandy palm of little Charlotte Cook.

Charlotte stood almost to the top of Megan's long legs. She was five and the only daughter of the Cooks in beach hut 501. For most of the time Megan thought she was cute with her tomboy basin haircut, but Charlotte was becoming increasingly annoying this summer. She had become Megan's shadow – everywhere Megan went, Charlotte was there. They were beach hut neighbours and very nosy – not always great to have around when Megan's grandparents' beach hut 502, better known as Parry, was anything but your regular Bexhill-on-Sea beach hut. Megan and her brother Marcus often needed to watch out for the Cooks and make sure their family secret about beach hut Parry was kept safe.

'I found it behind your beach hut,' Charlotte said.

Brushing her long strawberry-blonde curls aside, Megan looked casually over her shoulder toward Parry, sitting clean, tidy and pale grey amongst the row of beach huts.

'Well, it is beautiful, Charlotte,' Megan replied; 'but you can't keep something as precious as that. Whoever it belongs to will want it back.'

Charlotte clasped the ring tightly into her palm. 'My dad always says: "Finders-keepers", so I'm keeping it.'

Typical, Megan thought. Mr Cook carried his metal detector around all the time, like a surfer with his surfboard. Megan remembered that her Gran had once told her that she had left her radio on the beach and by the time she had returned back to fetch it, Mr Cook was already looking it over and opening his big shoulder bag to pocket it. Now, looking at Charlotte so fiercely holding the ring, Megan wasn't so sure the Cooks would hand it in to the police.

Marcus stepped out of the beach hut, closing the aqua-green wooden door behind him with a loud bang and came toward the girls. He was used to seeing Megan frowning whenever Charlotte was around. This time was no different. Thank goodness, he thought, there was no one around to bother him this summer. The weather had been warm and sunny and annoying kids could stay well out of his way. Sunburn was the only hindrance he was having – his milky-white skin barely ever tanned. Yet, with a long white shirt on and his Spiderman cap on top of his surfie's longish blonde hair, he thought himself well protected.

'Well, you can't keep it,' Megan continued. 'You can get into big trouble if you do.' Charlotte bowed her head, looking down at the brilliant diamond and rubbing her grubby thumb all over it.

'Cool! Charlotte,' Marcus interrupted. 'That sure is awesome. You will probably get a big reward from the owner once you hand it in. Do you want me to look after it for you and take it to the police?' As he stretched out his pale-skinned hand to accept the ring, Charlotte jumped back and ran off with the ring inside her small fist.

'Come back, Charlotte!' Megan cried.

Marcus laughed. 'You want Charlotte now? I thought you wanted some time to yourself.'

Hands on her hips, watching Charlotte running down the pebbly beach, Megan shook her head. 'That diamond is real, Marcs, and must be worth thousands of pounds. We'll need to get her to give it to the police.' She walked off around the back of Parry. There was just enough room between the back of Parry and the reinforcement wall; the promenade's footpath was just above it – at eye level they could see the holiday-makers' flip-flops shuffling along at summer pace.

'What are you doing, Megs?' Marcus asked, following behind.

'Charlotte found it around here,' she said. 'I am wondering if…' But Megan couldn't finish what she was about to say – both of the children could faintly hear Parry's alarm from inside; EP was calling them and that could only mean one thing – big trouble.

Chapter Two

As he slammed the door shut, one of the white-washed wooden paddles fell off the wall, hitting Marcus on the head. Inside the beach hut, Parry's alarm flashed a red light. Megan went to press the green button to stop the alarm sound and light.

'What is it, Parry? What does EP need?' she asked. Parry only ever sounded the alarm when EP, the secret organisation that stands for the Environmental Protection of World Beaches, needed their help.

'Is it the secret beach mission?' Marcus asked. He knew that was impossible without having EP's highest rank of White Swan, but he so hoped for it.

'Not this time, Marcus,' Parry said. 'My records tell me you are still three ranks from such a mission, but as EP agents you know it is your duty to protect all world-famous beaches from catastrophic environmental crimes.' It was true – last summer EP had sent them to protect

Whitehaven Beach in Australia and following that, all through the boring music and maths classes at school, they had both been daydreaming of going back there one day – to roll in the powdery soft white sand. Megan and Marcus also thought that travelling in Parry was better than they could imagine first-class seats to be on British Airways!

'I know, Parry,' Marcus said. 'You know I have to ask anyway. We will go anywhere with you.' Parry, Megan and Marcus were like a team. Parry had been working as an undercover vessel, transporting the Morgan family EP agents to far-away beaches in an instant and had been doing so for about fifty years – as long as all the generations of children of the Morgan family had been working for EP. It was a cool job – dangerous, secretive – but very cool.

'That's right, Parry,' Megan said. 'After all, your name is Paradise, or as we affectionately call you – Parry. Says it all – we love going and rescuing paradise beaches.'

'Why thank you,' Parry said. 'It is a

pleasure and a duty to work alongside both of you. Speaking of which, EP seeks your immediate departure to Hanauma Bay in Hawaii.'

Marcus turned the red and navy lifebuoy clockwise that hung on the wall, releasing a map from a hidden panel beside it. It showed the exact location of Hanauma Bay.

'Here it is,' he said. 'It is pronounced Ha-now-ma Bay and it's on the island of O'ahu, right?' he said, pointing at the south-east corner of the island.

'That's correct, Marcus,' Parry answered. 'It is the most developed of the Hawaiian Islands. That means there are lots of people and buildings there. In Hawaiian it is known as 'The Gathering Place.' Megan and Marcus glanced at each other with that sense of sparky excitement they always got before heading off on a beach-saving mission. They sat down in the candy-striped deck chairs and looked toward the alarm box to continue listening to Parry.

'The island lives up to its name – it was one of the first islands in the world that made tourists dream of going on a tropical holiday. Thousands of people go to O'ahu every year, which makes some parts of the island very busy,' Parry explained.

'Like Bexhill-on-Sea on a really hot day?' Marcus said smiling. There had been lots of day trippers to Bexhill this summer. The children had never seen it so crowded and had to lay out their towels in front of Parry, just to guard some space on the beach to enjoy.

'Even busier than Bexhill-on-Sea, Marcus,' Parry answered. 'Imagine a beach so popular that it has to restrict the number of people and charge for entry to the beach. That is Hanauma Bay. It has three thousand visitors per day. It is closed to the public on Tuesdays to let the fish eat and swim in peace.'

Megan leaned forward to look at the map as it focused in on Hanauma Bay. 'It sounds like tourists love it.'

'Precisely, Megan,' Parry said. 'That is just the problem – it is being loved to death. An EP contact awaits our arrival.

Prepare for immediate departure.'

Megan wrapped an orange cotton scarf around her neck as beach hut travel was quick, but quite chilly. They strapped the boat garland that was strung on white-washed twine, across their laps. It transformed into highly-secure seat belts. Putting on their caps, they rubbed the peaks. The caps transformed into hi-tech helmets. Marcus took hold of the lifebuoy and pressing the rope knot on one side, released its control panel. He entered the destination – Hanauma Bay, Hawaii.

'Well, Megs,' he said. 'We are following in the footsteps of Grandad.' He put a pair of socks on for the flight to keep himself warm.

'We are?' Megan said.

Marcus nodded.

'Grandad told me that Hawaii was his last mission as an EP agent. He turned nineteen just after his return home and retired from EP service.'

Megan grinned at the thought of going to Hawaii just like Grandad. 'Did he have a blast of a time?' she asked.

Marcus' face turned stone cold. 'He said it was the most dangerous mission of his entire life.'

Megan's grin disappeared. Visors down and hands clasping the deck-chair with feet firmly planted on Parry's wooden floorboards, they lifted off for the beautiful, but deadly, Hanauma Bay.

Chapter Three

In super beach-hut speed, they arrived two minutes later. Parry touched down as light as a feather. Megan took the 'Gone to the beach' arrow sign off the wall, and felt down its side for the on switch. The old wooden sign transformed into a mini-computer. Its screen gave a clear picture of the outside. Hanauma Bay curved like a breakfast cereal bowl with gentle sapphire blue waves lapping at the edges; its water glistened in the morning sun.'There is hardly anyone here,' Marcus observed. 'Parry, this is Hanauma Bay?'

'Affirmative, Marcus,' Parry replied. 'We are approximately ten miles east of Waikiki Beach and situated in the far end of the parking lot for Hanauma Bay. Local time is ten past six in the morning. Opening times are 6 a.m. to 7 p.m. The Number 22 Bus from Waikiki will arrive shortly with the first of the day trippers. The parking lot will be full before midday. I have secured a spot that is overgrown with trees and branches. My invisible shield is on, so please use your night vision goggles to find me.'

'Thanks as always, Parry,' Megan said. She undid her seatbelt and grabbed the new orange and yellow crocheted and beaded beach bag that her Gran had made. She reached inside it for her waterproof bag. She would need to take her valuable devices with her everywhere – even in the water. 'Ready, Marcs?' Marcus was busy rubbing in sun-cream on his face. Unlike Megan, Marcus' skin was incredibly milky-white and he was forever slapping on sun-cream.

'Ready', he said.

They opened the beach hut door and stepped down on to the sandy dirt ground. The air was calm and warm for so early in the morning. There were a dozen or so cars already parked up. Some people were preparing their snorkelling equipment. Others were draping beach towels and cameras around their necks. A few were drinking the last of their coffees and admiring the bay. Parry was invisible to the naked eye. Megan and Marcus casually walked toward the ticket booth, but didn't get far.

'It's as cold as ice, hey?' A large, dark-haired and dark-tanned Hawaiian guy said. His smile was so wide, and he flashed the whitest of teeth. His rainbow-coloured shirt was long and he wore silver rings on most fingers. Marcus shook hands and felt his knuckles nearly break with the guy's strength.

'Three feet of ice does not result from one day of cold weather,' Marcus replied. EP's secret passwords had always been ridiculous for exotic beaches of the world, but saying this old Chinese proverb at Hanauma Bay was simply stupid.

'Good journey, Marcus? Aloha! Megan.' He placed a purple lei around both their necks. 'This is the customary welcome when arriving in Hawaii,' he said.

'Hi, Lio and thanks,' they both said. Megan smelt the deep perfume from the lei.

'You kids need to upgrade your photos

14

to EP,' he said. 'You must be about a foot taller, right?' It was true. Over the summer, they had both grown and were more and more becoming tall, thin and lanky − a trait of the Morgan family. Neither of them minded. They were both in tall classes at school, so it felt normal. Megan suspected that it was sure to help on some of their EP missions, too.

'Come over to my van so we don't stand out,' Lio said. His combi van was bright orange with peace symbol stickers and dangly chimes on the inside rear view mirror. Megan wondered just how much of it was a disguise and how much was actually Lio.

Lio read her mind. 'It is actually me, babe,' he said to Megan. 'Lived in Hawaii all my life; I might work for EP, but I'm what you might call a 'casual' employee. They needed someone who knew Hawaii like the back of his own hand − well that was me. But I can't ever leave this place, so I work for EP only in Hawaii.'

'Did you ever work with our Grandfather?' Marcus asked.

'No offence, Marcus, but I'm not that

old,' he said, with a smile. 'I do know about that mission – it was a famous one for EP. Your Grandfather became a legend for his bravery in saving a beach on the Big Island.'

Marcus knew just as much and had seen the Garuda medal hidden once in his Grandfather's study. It was the highest order given to EP agents. More cars were arriving and the car park was filling up. The queue at the ticket booth to gain entry was getting longer.

'So let's get down to business,' Lio said, sitting on the edge of his van. 'There is a pile-up of rubbish going on here and it needs cleaning up.' He leant into his van and pulled out a small bag of litter – cigarette butts, beer cans, burger wrappers, flavoured milk cartons, screwed-up crisp packets, ice cream cones and sticks and an array of other sour-smelling used food and drink packaging.

'EP has been called in to clean up a beach?' Megan said. She couldn't believe her eyes or ears. Surely cleaning the beach was a job for the local council?

It hardly seemed the sort of job that top EP agents would be left to solve.

'Well, Megan,' Lio replied. 'Don't judge the rubbish by its wrapper – if you know what I mean. This is no ordinary littering.'

'What do you mean?' Marcus asked.

Lio leant in and picked up a stinking old flavoured-milk carton. He turned it over and stuck to it was a brochure about Hanauma Bay. What caught their attention was the angry red writing that someone had scrawled across the brochure. It read, 'Die, Hanauma Bay!' As Lio sorted through the rubbish, copies of the same brochure came to the surface. They all had the same message.

'So you are suggesting there is a plot to destroy Hanauma Bay?' Megan asked.

'Exactamundo, Megan,' Lio answered. 'EP has been called in after several large deposits of rubbish have landed mysteriously on the beach at Hanauma Bay. No-one has seen anyone do it, but it takes three truck loads to get rid of the rubbish and each time it happens, there is more and more. What's more – this message suggests a very real danger for the Bay and all living on it and in it. It's starting to get into the water and when it does that, it will strangle the marine life.' Lio poured bottled water over his hands and shut the van door. Marcus was pleased to be able to breathe the clean air again.

'EP needs you to find out who is doing it and to stop it,' he continued. 'I will be your contact whenever you need me – day or night.' He handed them his mobile phone number.

'Is that it? Marcus said. 'Don't you have any special gadgets specific to this mission? Lio reached in his pocket and threw a small bottle of antiseptic hand gel to Marcus.

'You'll need that for sure,' he said. 'Rubbish is never clean and there's plenty of it on this job.'

Megan and Marcus thanked Lio and looked toward the ticket booth. It was time to get on to the beach and begin their search. Whoever was doing it was more than just an annoying litter lout. No, he or she had plans to totally destroy the environment. Looking out across the magnificent Hanauma Bay, Megan and Marcus could only think of one thing – in this beach mission, they would be dealing with pure evil.

Chapter Four

The queue moved quickly. Megan and Marcus didn't pay for entry as under 13-year-olds were free. A short film was shown inside the Marine Education Centre about the caring and protection of Hanauma Bay. Walking toward the entry for the beach, Megan and Marcus noticed how much the visitors took note and showed respect for the environment. They watched the film, asked questions about what they were allowed to do and read the rules for being at Hanauma Bay. Nobody looked suspicious or out of place there. Marcus walked over toward the board that listed the beach rules.

'Take a look at this, Megs,' he said. 'Five Points to Protect Hanauma Bay Nature Preserve. One: Stand only on sand. Two: Observe, but don't touch the reef. Three: Watch the fish, but don't feed them. Four: Do not litter. Five: Use the restrooms before you swim.'

Megan nodded. 'It all sounds okay,' she said. 'Particularly the rule about not peeing in the water – that is such a gross thing to do.'

Just as they were standing there, a loud tour guide's voice was overheard. She was saying: '…so no swimming in the toilet bowls! Right everyone? They are dangerous places.'

Megan spun around to the tour guide who had just finished the tour and stopped her.

'Excuse me,' she said. 'What toilet bowl are you referring to?'

The tour guide had a cheery round face and wore a name tag that said: 'Alanna'.

'Not the kind of toilet bowl you are probably thinking of,' she said with a big strong American accent from the South. 'Toilet bowls are like large tide pools carved into the rocks and water comes in a force, swishing all about – like a toilet bowl flush,' she said. 'Be sure not to go in there and stick to the safer swimming and snorkeling areas. Have you got your snorkeling gear or will you young people be hiring?'

'Hire if we can,' Marcus answered. 'Is

it worth doing?'

'Is it worth doin'?' Alanna almost shouted. 'Is my Mama's apple pie worth eating? Why, of course it is. By the sounds of your English accents, I would say it is definitely worth travelling thousands of miles and doin' – you can see the world's most beautiful, but threatened, green sea-turtles out there if you're lucky – but don't go touching, chasing or feeding them if you meet them, 'cause that would be against the law, ya hear?'

Megan and Marcus thanked her and began walking to the snorkel hire.

'Hey,' Alanna called to them. 'Sounds like you might benefit from a tour of mine. I'm running one in an hour or so. Give you time to have a snorkel and meet me down on the beach.'

That was exactly what they needed – an expert to tell them about the Bay.

'Thanks,' Megan said. 'We'll be there.'

The beach was clean; sandy and with some grass, it was only about half a mile long. There was not one stray chocolate wrapper, empty crisp pack or crushed soft drink can to be seen. It was almost hard to believe that EP had a case to solve on such a beautiful beach. But EP agents often knew that the best beaches in the world looked as if nothing was wrong – until you began to scratch the surface.

Marcus noticed the small mouth of the Bay to the ocean. The coral reef was large. He was well aware that it provided plenty of protection against large waves and big fish, like sharks or dolphins. It was a wonderful safe playground to explore – he just had to remember it was an EP mission and danger could be lurking anywhere at any moment in time.

Megan put her bag down and took off her sundress. She was wearing her new purple EP agent swimming suit. It looked like any other girls' swimsuit, but sewn into its sides were secret devices – a super thin pocket-knife and a high-powered torch-light. She just needed to undo the side zipper and she could use them when needed.

Marcus either tore or grew out of his swimming trunks every few months.

Parry seemed to have a never-ending supply of new EP trunks in the Beach Hut. He wore a knee-length turquoise blue pair with guitars and palm trees on them – his favourite ones so far. Knife and torch-light were also secretly sewn in the side seams. He took off his shirt and cap and began pulling on his snorkel, goggles and fins. It was much easier to go to the water and slip on the fins, but Marcus had his own way of doing things. This usually meant a clumsier way – he kicked up sand as he walked knees-to-chest to the water. Passers-by smiled at him, most likely wondering if he had ever snorkelled before. On the contrary, he had done a lot of snorkelling – he just didn't look as if he had.

Meanwhile, Megan was already snorkelling in the crystal clear waters. As she looked down, she saw that the reef was like an underwater city with all sorts of animals and plants living there. Gliding along above the coral bed, she could see the lobe, cauliflower and rice blue corals alive everywhere. Dozens of tiny colourful tropical fish darted passed her goggles and into crevices between the coral formations and the rocks. A few slightly larger fish to her right were feeding off the algae growing in the water. A busy crab stomped back to his home as if annoyed at the passing traffic of fish so close to his front door. A gentle wave motion slightly shifted Megan to view more coral. Then something else caught her attention. It was swaying like the plant life rising up from the coral beds but, it wasn't a plant. It was litter − a chocolate wrapper firmly planted as part of the coral reef. It must have washed into the water. The morning sun made its silver side shine bright. It was Megan's first sight of the crime happening in Hanauma Bay.

Marcus had joined Megan and also saw the litter. It was small in contrast to the vast amounts of coral growth in the Bay, but it was there all the same. They drifted further away enjoying the show of fish and plant life. The morning sun warmed their backs and the water was warm enough not to feel the least bit cold. The coral continued to sway like wet hair in a bathtub. The sea floor was a mix of sand and coral. They stayed afloat, careful not to touch anything. A parrot fish, a trumpet fish and even an angel fish were sighted. Marcus was hoping to see the Hawaiian state fish – a reef trigger fish called humuhumunu-kunukuapua'a. To be able to see one would be great, let alone actually say its name!

However, time was going fast and they had drifted quite a way. Both were aware Alanna's tour was soon to start. Apart from one wrapper, nothing appeared unusual. That is, until they turned to paddle back to shore. Expecting to see more animal and plant life, they instead paddled straight into a sunken box full of nothing but litter. Its lid had become unfastened and strewn pieces of rubbish waved slowly out of the box, as if calling out to be rescued. On one side of the box, it had the same words that Lio had earlier shown – 'Die, Hanauma Bay!' Megan's skin shivered at the sight of it. Just how it got there, they had no idea, but sure enough, they had gone beneath

26

the surface of Hanaumu Bay and found that something was definitely up. It was time to come up from the water, get dry and get down to the bottom of this crime. If more of this litter landed here, the Bay could be choked to death in a matter of days.

Chapter Five

There were three other people on the tour. One – an older man, with grey hair and a beard – was an environmental historian, researching the beaches of Hawaii.

'Hi, Wally Brecon's the name,' he said to the group, shaking hands with everyone. 'I'm visiting on behalf of the University of Iowa. I am interested in how the plant and animal life survive here with so many visitors to the Bay – that's approximately 1.2 million visitors per year, which breaks down to 100,000 per month and is roughly 3,300 per day on average.' Wally kept reeling off facts and figures, which made Alanna begin to look a little dizzy with just all the stuff he knew. Marcus made a mental note to talk to him after the tour and find out what else he knew about Hanauma Bay.

An older teenager, who Marcus thought obviously liked to eat food a lot, was asked to put away his hamburger. He did so, but not as Alanna had instructed. He ate it in two massive bites and licked the ketchup off his over-sized Red Sox T-shirt.

'Oh, hi,' he said. 'I'm Travis Taylor and I'm on vacation with my Grandma. She doesn't do beaches much, so dropped me off. I don't really get into beaches either, but thought I'd kill a couple of hours here and take a look around.' He wiped his hands across his shirt and Megan noticed just how grotty his clothes and the palms of his hands were. She couldn't imagine traveling around with her own Grandma looking as grubby as he did. Grandma Morgan loved the idea of kids being kids, but stopped short of heavy dirt and grime. It made her wonder what his Grandma looked like.

The other tourist was a woman who said she made films and was interested to come to the place where many famous films and TV shows had been made. Her silvery-blonde hair was swept up and Megan suspected it had the contents of a full can of hairspray keeping it firmly in place. She was unlikely to be going snorkelling and getting wet.

'Hi, I'm Hilary McRoy,' she said. She almost sang her name as her voice was high-pitched – almost squeaky. Her arms jangled to the sound and weight of chunky bracelets on narrow wrists. She reminded Marcus of some sort of musical instrument, clanking and clinking. 'Oh yes,' she continued. 'Elvis Presley starred in Blue Hawaii and was filmed here back in the 1960s. Hawaii Five-O – the original series was filmed here, as was Magnum P.I.' She sighed seeming a bit lost in time and then began to rapidly take photos of the Bay and everyone around her. Everyone except for Wally Brecon also looked a bit lost – they were all too young to even know who or what she was talking about. The rest of the group looked toward Megan and Marcus, waiting to hear their reasons for visiting.

'We are on our holidays and love to come to the beach.' It was innocent and true enough. No-one asked where their parents were – they were looking old enough these days not to be asked.

'Nice to meet y'all,' Alanna began, 'and welcome to y'all – to the best beach in the USA. That's right – Hanauma Bay has been voted the best beach 'cause of its warm clean water and sand, how well kept the beach is, litter control and its facilities. As you can see, there are picnic areas, shady areas, freshwater showers, restrooms, pay phones, a gift shop, wheelchair access and our great educational information centre.'The group all looked around and saw how well-organised it was for a beach.

Alanna continued, 'Our biggest achievements though, are our protection of the plant and animal life in the water.

'But it wasn't always that way, was it?' Wally interrupted.

'No siree,' Alanna said. 'Back in the 1980s there were as many as 13,000 visitors a day to Hanuama Bay. It's safe to say that a lot of those tourists didn't have the foggiest about how fragile the marine ecosystem was and they caused a lot of problems – they trod and crushed the coral, dropped trash, fed the fish and left oil slicks of suntan lotion on the surface of the water. The Bay began to die from overuse, so things had to change for the better – and they did. Limited numbers of tourists a day and a centre to teach people about how special the place is and what to do to keep it so pretty, has made a big difference.'

There was a break in the tour to take some more photos. Wally's binoculars were steadily focused on the area of water where Megan and Marcus had found the box of litter. Marcus wondered if Wally could see the litter. He seemed to be focused on it for some time.

Travis went to the rubbish bin to get rid of his hamburger wrapper and stood staring down into it. 'Geez,' he said, peering down into the bin. 'Even the bin is sparkly clean – you sure I can put my rubbish in there?'

Alanna nodded. Hilary McRoy clapped her strappy high-heeled sandals around the room making mention of the exact locations of where the filming had taken place.

'My documentary of the Bay will film all of these historic locations,' she said.

'You'll be needing permission, y'hear, Ms McRoy,' Alanna said, 'if you are gonna do any filming of that sort. They stopped that sort of thing a long time back to protect Hanauma Bay.' They began to get into a long discussion about the rules again. The tour was just about to re-start when loud voices and cries came from the locker hire area. Alanna and her group immediately followed the sound of the chaos.

'What's going on?' Alanna barged into the crowd that was gathered – more like a police officer than a tour guide. The security guard to the centre came over at once. He was thickset and about six feet tall.

As they all stood around, they could see several tourists had opened the lockers and filthy, stinking litter was pouring out in mounds and filling the area with the vilest smell. Hands covered noses everywhere.

'Pooh! It stinks!' voices shrieked out. The security guard went to investigate the other lockers and opened them. Every single one of the lockers was full to the brim with the same litter – food and drink rubbish. Instantly, the litter fell out and grew into a massive mound of stench. Tourists began coughing and running out of the centre to escape the foul smell and ugliness of it. Just when everyone had left the locker area and was outside getting fresh air, shouts and cries started up again. Alanna and the security guard were still rubbing their heads at all the litter that was in front of them.

'Oh! What now?' Alanna said, moving fast toward the crowd gathered outside. Megan and Marcus followed close behind.

There was an even bigger crowd of people around the side of the education centre. People were stunned and now standing silently, shaking their heads at what had happened. Megan and Marcus pushed through the crowd until they were face to face with what had stunned the crowd. Right in front of them was the worst message of all. They had seen it before, but now it was shocking as it covered the side wall. In big, sloppy red spray-paint, the graffiti read: 'Die! Hanauma Bay!'

'Hey! Down here!' Travis Taylor was down on the beach and calling out for some help. The security guard, Alanna, Wally Brecon and even Hilary McRoy, with her shoes now off, ran down to join him. Megan and Marcus were right behind. Others too began to run down on to the beach. Travis was standing still looking down at the sand. They all stood silent. It was the same message again but this time it had been written into the sand: 'Die! Hanauma Bay!'

Five minutes later the police had arrived and Hanauma Bay was closed.

'We better get back to Parry,' Marcus said. Megan nodded and together they ran, as the police taped off the beach.

Chapter Six

Back at Parry's, Megan and Marcus searched the computer screen for unusual activity at the Bay. Parry's closed circuit TV was able to film the surrounding area from the time they had left earlier in the day.

'Insufficient reach,' Parry said. 'My camera cannot film that far away. I have informed EP of this fault.' Parry was incredibly proud of his capabilities and he became annoyed when he couldn't do what EP agents needed him to do.

'That's not your fault, Parry,' Megan said. 'EP should be working on these latest technologies for you. They have been incredibly slow of late, to get you fitted out with them.'

Marcus could sense Parry feeling less than perfect, which was not a feeling that sat well with a robotic agent.

'We will do fine without it, Parry,' he said. 'Don't worry. But you could help us out with detecting traces of anything, in this sample of rubbish. Perhaps you

could let us know where it came from.'
Marcus fed the dirty litter into the chute
below Parry's voice box mounted on the
wall. Parry's testing of the litter would
take enough time for Marcus to use Lio's
hand gel and get rid of the smell and
germs that were on his hands.
Meanwhile, Megan kept scanning the
closed circuit footage and zoomed in on
something unusual.

'Take a look at this, Marcs,' she said.
The camera zoomed in on a parked van
in the parking lot. Its side curtains parted
slightly and they could just make out that
a whole lot of junk was inside the van.
What made Megan and Marcus so
interested was Travis Taylor leaning into
the back of the van. They could
recognise him because of his Red-Sox
T-shirt and baggy shorts, which hung so
low that his ugly white butt poked out. It
was difficult to see clearly, but he looked
as if he was tying something up. He then
shut the back door of the van, holding
another hamburger in his hand and
lumbered off toward the education
centre. The film footage was captured

just about the time that the tour was to start. The van remained parked for about five more minutes and then left in the direction of the centre.'Try zooming in on the driver, Megs,' Marcus said, staring with his nose nearly touching the screen.

The camera went in as far as it could, but all they could see were gloved hands on the steering wheel. It was too hard to see who was driving the van.

'Odd vehicle for a grandmother, isn't it? I mean he said that he was on vacation with her, right?' Marcus said.

Megan wondered – she wouldn't have put it past their grandmother; when she was a bit younger – she was known as the 'hippy grandma' of Bexhill. Colourful kaftans, headscarves and loads of big beads draped around her neck, were her thing – and she still greeted friends in the street with a two-fingered V peace sign.

'Perhaps his gran is the mother earth type,' Megan replied. 'And he did say she wasn't into the beach scene, which could explain why she didn't hang around for long.' Megan kept on looking at the recorded film footage. 'But here's something interesting, Marcs.' Parry's camera had managed to capture Hilary McRoy at the parking ticket vending machine. There was nothing strange about that – but the fact that she was having an enormous argument with Wally Brecon, the historian, did look very strange.

'Something tells me they're not arguing over having change for a parking ticket,' Marcus said. The film couldn't pick up on what they were arguing about, but Hilary seemed totally mad – flapping her arms about and shouting – nothing like the sophisticated woman they had met on the tour.

'Well, whatever it is,' Megan said, 'It looks like they know each other – look Wally put his hand on her arm to calm her down. Yet they didn't seem to be together on the tour – they were like strangers with each other.'

They kept watching the film of tourists arriving, parking their cars, getting their beach gear out and wandering over to the ticket entrance – loads of tourists and from what they could make out, barely any locals. It was going to be important to talk to the locals to understand something more about the Bay. Tourists come and go, but the locals would be the ones that could see anything unusual going on. Or maybe someone that knew the Bay like they were local.

They must have both been thinking this at the same time, as they said together, 'We need to talk to Alanna.' It was a tour guide's job to know absolutely everything about the place they ran tours in. Alanna had to know more than just the facts and history of the Bay.

Parry spoke up. 'I have analysed the litter sample,' he said.

'Yes, Parry,' Megan said. 'Did you find any clues?'

Parry's voice box released a piece of paper with the results of his analysis.

Marcus scanned it and read aloud, 'Traces of glue on wrapper, wet, with particles of mountain soil.'

'Mountain soil…?' Megan was puzzled. 'How can you tell, Parry?'

'Its colour, richness and feel,' he replied. 'Given its freshness, it may not be from far away.'

'A rubbish dump, perhaps?' Marcus suggested.

'It is quite possible,' Parry replied. 'But the rubbish has not been rubbish for long – it has not decomposed as they say. It may have been stored somewhere else.'

Megan grabbed her camera. 'Let's get going, Marcus,' she said. 'If the rubbish keeps piling up as fast as we are seeing, Hanauma Bay could be destroyed within a matter of days. I'll check in with Alanna and find out what she knows about the littering. Why don't you see what Wally Brecon is up to? I think he knows something.'

Marcus picked up his cap. 'Definitely,' he said. 'Let's get out there.'

Chapter Seven

Megan and Marcus split up in the car park. They agreed to meet on the beach at midday. The sun was much warmer and there seemed to be three times the number of tourists than earlier in the morning. Megan walked toward the education centre in search of Alanna. Crowds were gathered around with puzzled looks. The police were still keeping the beach taped off, as they were photographing the message written in the sand. The centre was also closed to the general public. Megan tried to squeeze through the crowd and while the security guard was not looking, she slid quietly through the glass door. The smell of rubbish hit her hard – it was as if she had stuck her head inside a full rubbish bin and kept it there. It made her want to be sick. Alanna was near the lockers helping a cleaner tidy up the mess, so Megan made her way over.

'Happy to help if I can,' Megan said, reaching for a broom. She began to sweep with it, but the rubbish wouldn't budge.

'That's awful kind of ya, Miss,' Alanna said. 'But ya can't move the stuff without a scraper.' She was scraping at the mound of rubbish that had glued itself to the highly- polished floor.

'Anyway,' she went on. 'You aren't supposed to be in here – the centre is closed to the public right now. You come back when it opens up, y'hear?' She arched her back, aching from the strain of bending down for so long.

'I know,' Megan said, 'but more hands make light work, my Gran always says. My name's Megan by the way.' She spotted a spare pair of hygiene gloves, put them on and set to work picking at the stuck rubbish. Reaching in the side pocket of her swimmers, she pulled out her knife and used the blunt side to peel the rubbish from the floor.

'Well, I could get in trouble,' Alanna said. 'But you are right about how much work there is to do. So I thank you for your help. Just stay out of the way of the police.' She pointed over to two officers who were making their way slowly over toward the locker area. It seemed that Megan wasn't going to have to ask Alanna too many questions after all – she would be able to listen in to her talk with the police officers.

'As I said last time y'all were here,' Alanna said, as she scraped the rubbish off the floor, 'someone's not liking our conservation restrictions and they want to dump their dirt all over us in protest. Those older Kama'aina probably have some special memories of the way it used to be here – what with camping out, fishing and spearing hundreds of fish. They're not gonna like the new rules to protect the Bay. They can't come here in crowds, can't smoke on the beach, have to pay to get on to the beach and can't fish. Well, they have their noses put right out with all this protection of the Bay – so they figure our noses should smell all this 'ere stench.'

Megan busied herself by scraping inside a locker. She didn't want to be told to leave. The police officers kept asking Alanna more questions, but she didn't have much more to tell.

'Nope,' she said. 'I didn't see anyone around here – just tourists.' They thanked her and walked away to question the security guard.

'Alanna,' Megan said. 'Who is the Kama'aina?'

Alanna tied a refuse bag up and threw it in the corner with the others.

'Kama'aina,' she said, 'is a person who has lived for a long time in Hawaii. They sometimes move away, but they are, as you say, a "child of the land."'

'Do you think a Kama'aina has done this because they don't want people to protect this place? That seems mad.'

'People have funny ideas of what is good for others and for places too,' she said. 'If there had not been any conservation rules made, Hanauma Bay would have died thirty years ago.'

'But now this message about wanting Hanauama Bay to die,' Megan said. 'It's as if the very place that they loved to come to, they want to destroy. That doesn't make sense.'

Alanna wiped her hands with hand gel

and a paper towel. The locker area was nearly cleaned up.

'When does breaking the law ever make sense? Now, I think we deserve a nice cold drink. Let me buy you one, for all the good work you've done here and I can tell you where you should take a walk to see the best of Hanauma Bay. Seeing as you can't get down on the beach right now.' Megan followed and enjoyed the cold orangeade from the machine.

'You see that hiking trail over there? It's the Koko Head loop. It takes you out along the rim of the Bay.' Alanna said. 'Take that along the ridge. It overlooks the Bay and you will be blown away by such an amazing view.'

Megan had time to do that before meeting Marcus at midday. She thanked Alanna and headed off, putting her cap on to shield her head from the hot sun. Megan climbed the steep walkway with safety rails. She left the crowds behind and before too long was off the paved trail and had made it to the top near the radio stations. She stared over the sparkling blue and turquoise Hanauma Bay. The view was all the way from Diamond Point to Makapau Point and with the sun directly overhead it was hot to stand there for long.

Megan decided to climb down the rocks toward the beach. There were green ropes along the ledge, but all of a sudden she found that she had wandered on to a private reserve area and had left the trail. Looking from left to right, she saw no one around and was figuring out how to get back on the trail, when she noticed another of the gluey sticky wrappers stuck to her flip-flop. Bending down to remove it, she saw more wrappers drifting along the top of the rocks toward a clustering of low-lying shrubs. Megan moved toward them to see exactly where they were coming from. Parting the shrubs to look into the clearing, she gasped. Right before her was what looked like a small rubbish tip. It must have been where all the rubbish was coming from. There were mounds of tightly-packed rubbish organised in a neat formation of rows. She saw what looked like a cauldron that was steaming and overflowing with a glue-like substance. There was a caravan hidden under the shrubbery – well-camouflaged from passers-by. Megan moved in closer, but tripped on a wire that sounded the clinking of empty soft-drink cans.

Getting to her feet, a breeze picked up and nearly blew her over again. It set off the alarm of rubbish chiming for someone to hear. Untangling herself from the wire, she got to her feet once more and sprinted out of sight, before anyone could catch her. She had to get back to Marcus and tell him what she had found. Alanna was right – she did get blown away by what she saw – but it wasn't the view of Hanauma Bay. Moving faster down the hill, no one saw her, or at least, that was what she thought. Something stirred in the shrubs above and whatever it was took a long hard look at Megan running away.

Chapter Eight

Marcus was among the tourists, watching the police photograph the threat written in the sand down on the beach. Without any more evidence, the beach was soon re-opened and the tourists poured down the steep hill to sit under the palm trees or were heading straight out to snorkel in the sea. Wally Brecon was nowhere to be seen, so Marcus decided to take a wander around the other side of the education centre. It was shaded and cool out of the sun. The rubbish bags had been gathered waiting for the pick-up truck. He took some photos of the rubbish bags on his iPhone and sent them to Parry.

'I wouldn't be standing around near that garbage,' a high-pitched female voice said. Marcus turned; it was Hilary McRoy. She had changed clothes and had shorts, T-shirt, trainers and visor on. A camera and tripod were slung over her shoulder and her ear-phones were dangling around her neck.

'I was just taking a look around,' Marcus answered. 'What about you? What are you doing?'

'Same as you,' she said, 'but with a documentary to make, I thought I might film some of this latest drama – what with all the rubbish and threats written on the beach, I think it might make a riveting start to it. Now if you can kindly move to the side, so I can film some of this rubbish.'

'I thought you needed permission from the Centre to film anything around here,' Marcus said. Hilary took no notice and started filming all the rubbish and around the back of the Centre. She wandered away, leaving Marcus standing there alone.

A van pulled up and the rubbish was loaded into the back of it. A big guy with tattoos down both his arms jumped out of the van and hoisted the bags into the back. Marcus took a few more photos of the guy loading the rubbish and again sent them to Parry. The guy had just about finished loading the van, when the last big refuse bag cut his hand.

'Ouch!' he screeched. 'What on earth…' His palm had a cut and he reached for a cloth in the van to stop the bleeding. Marcus went over to see if he was all right. The bleeding was easing. He offered to put the bag into the van, but when he bent down he noticed the bag had been gashed open and the contents were starting to pour out. That's when Marcus saw that it wasn't just rubbish in the bag.

'Probably just a can of Coke,' the driver said. 'Sure didn't tickle.'

Marcus extracted the sharp object from the bag. 'No,' he said. 'I think you'll see it is coral that cut your hand.' He held out a vibrantly coloured piece of coral that was as sharp as Marcus' pocket knife.'I think I better take this inside to the police,' he said. 'It's not just rubbish, is it?

'That's coral from out in Hanauma Bay, most likely. I've got no idea why it's amongst this rubbish.'

Marcus started to walk toward the door to the Centre when an arm came around from behind, a hessian bag was thrown over his head and he was pushed into the van with the rest of the rubbish. The sliding door slammed shut. The motor started and in a split second he was thrust forward with all the rubbish.

'Hey! What do you think you are doing?' Marcus shouted. 'You have no right to do this to me.' Quickly, Marcus threw off the bag from his head, grabbed his iPhone and sent an urgent message to Parry. He told him he was in the van with the rubbish. A dark glass panel concealed the driver, so Marcus couldn't tell if it was the guy who had cut his hand or not. He had grabbed Marcus roughly – the sides of his ribs were hurting where he had been shoved into the van. Trying to open the door was hopeless as it and the side windows were all locked and blacked out. He kicked hard at the door, but it didn't budge. He searched his pocket for his cap and put it on. Rubbing its peak, it immediately transformed into a hi-tech helmet. Now with super x-ray vision, Marcus was able to see beyond the dark glass panel as far as the driver.

It was at this precise moment that the

driver looked up and smiled to the guy who had been collecting the rubbish who was next to him – it was Travis Taylor! He was laughing and smacking his hand on the steering wheel as he sped down the road. Marcus had no idea why they had thrown him in the back of the van and what Travis had to do with all of this, but he knew one thing – he had to get out of the van quick-smart before he ended up on top of a piled heap of rubbish. Keeping his helmet on, he felt for the side button and pressed it. A fine red laser light shot out toward the lock on the van door. He tried to steady himself as the van moved fast along the road. Making a circle with the red laser, he burnt through the lock and kicked it out of the way. Waiting for the van to make a slow turn into another road, he was able to push the door open and leapt like a frog into the bushes.

'Ow!' He said, rubbing his butt. He had landed on a prickly bush and it hurt. Zooming in his x-ray camera on the van, he was able to glimpse the number plate. Travis and the other guy hadn't even noticed that he had baled out. Marcus stayed hidden for a few moments longer until the van was way down the road.

His iPhone buzzed. It was Parry. 'Are you safe?'

Marcus replied, 'Yes'. He rubbed his side and checked if there were any thorns sticking into him, but there weren't. There was, however, a piece of the rubbish from the van stuck to his butt. He peeled it off and turned just in time to run across the road and catch the bus back. The bus was busy with more tourists heading for Hanauma Bay. Making his way to the back of the bus, he sat down and twisted the piece of rubbish in his hand. It was another chocolate wrapper. Whoever was throwing all of this rubbish on to Hanauma Bay, sure had eaten stacks of chocolate, he thought. But it was Travis Taylor who was really making him think. What was he up to? And why had he thrown Marcus into the van? There was nothing suspicious that Marcus had done to catch anyone's attention. Perhaps it was a random prank that Travis pulled on Marcus – trying to scare him. Parry would be able to help track the van's number plate and they could find out some more about the guy.

He jumped off the bus back at the Education Centre. Well past midday and there was no sign of Megan. It was time to get back to the beach hut.

Chapter Nine

Parry's voice box flashed and spat out a message from EP. It read, 'Solve this case as soon as possible. Hanauma Bay will be destroyed in a matter of days if the littering continues. Marine life has been injured in past week. Stop and find the criminals now.' The pressure was on to solve the case and everyone knew it. Megan and Marcus explained what had happened in the last hour or so. Megan began by telling about the mysterious caravan on the private reserve off the hiking trail and the boiling cauldron and mountains of rubbish. Marcus explained how Travis Taylor and some other big guy had pushed him into his van with rubbish that contained crushed coral.

'Now for my news,' Parry said. 'I have traced the number plate for you, Marcus, and it belongs to a woman by the name of Sue Taylor. She is a resident on O'ahu and is also Travis' grandmother.'

'That's great, Parry,' Marcus said. 'What about the other big guy that was with Travis? And you say his grandmother is a resident here – I thought Travis and his grandma were on holiday together?'

'No read as yet on Travis' accomplice,' Parry answered. 'Travis could be telling the truth, Marcus – he could be on holiday with his grandmother. He could be visiting her here.'

'What about the caravan up on the private reserve, Parry?' Megan asked. 'It was so weird seeing the caravan sitting there with a big boiling cauldron, like a witch's brew. I'm sure it definitely has something to do with whoever is dumping all the litter on Hanauma Bay.'

'It appears that we have struck a mystery up on the reserve,' Parry answered. 'When I transported myself to the area under the invisibility screen, it would seem that there was nothing of what you describe. The area was a reserve. I scanned for even the smallest scrap of litter, but found nothing.'

'So you're saying that what I saw up there wasn't there?' Megan shook her head. 'I know what I saw, Parry. It was definitely up there.' She turned back to Marcus. 'I'll need to go back up there and search around.'

Marcus nodded. 'Tomorrow will be perfect to do all this.' Megan looked puzzled and Marcus explained. 'Hanauma Bay is always closed to the public on Tuesdays. It lets the natural environment and all its marine life rest from the tourists – they can feed in peace. We will have the place to ourselves.'

'Yes, but we are the public in the eyes of everyone around here,' Megan said. 'How do you propose we get access back down onto the beach, near the Education Centre and up near the hiking trail? We will be marched right out of here, if Alanna finds us nosing around.'

'She is just the person we need to tell why we are here,' Marcus said. 'With her support we should be able to go everywhere we need to. For me, that is back out into the Bay to see what else is under the water. I'll also need to scan the beach for any further clues.'

'I want to get back up on that private

reserve and see what's going on,' Megan said, 'and back into the Education Centre. I need to learn some more about this area. Did you get to speak to Wally Brecon?'

'No,' Marcus said. 'I couldn't find him. I'll try now. Do you fancy having a shaved ice – Hawaii's version of a delicious ice lolly?'

Megan grabbed her drawstring bag and cap. 'Sure, that sounds perfect – it's hot out there,' she said. 'Let's go. We need to find out some more about Travis Taylor. I got the impression that Alanna knew him when we had the tour. I'll ask her.' Turning to face Parry's voice box, she asked, 'Will you remain stationed in this spot, Parry?'

'Yes,' Parry said. 'The car park is good for detecting who is coming and going. Speaking of which, agent Lio has arrived back and is standing near his car, three rows away.'

'Thanks, Parry,' Marcus said. 'Come on, Megs, let's check in with Lio before we do anything else.'

Chapter Ten

Lio was lazily leaning on his van, cleaning his snorkelling goggles.

'Ho! Howzit?' he said and gave Megan and Marcus a Hawaiian handshake. It meant 'hello' and 'what's up' in Hawaiian slang.

'Off to get some shaved ices', Marcus said.

Megan interrupted. 'And to speak to Alanna, the tour guide at the Centre – along with a few others who we think know more about what's going on.'

Lio let out a slow quiet whistle. 'Oh, shaved ice is so "ono",' he said. 'That's "delicious" in your language and Alanna, you say, she is, too – such a cool babe who knows a lot of stuff for someone not born here. She'll help you out. I'm wanting to ask her out, but it never seems to be the right time.' He sighed and put down his snorkelling gear and then placed his silver-ringed fingers on suntanned hips.

'But you've gotta know that EP are

stressing out a little about this one, guys,' he said. 'They are contacting me non-stop – wanting to know what you have done so far.' He flicked his wet hair and hopped on his left bare foot to rid water out of his ear. 'But hey, I don't want to tell you how to do your job. It's just that in the past hour, I've found even more of the rubbish dumped under water in the Bay. There's not a lot of time to solve this one without it becoming an international disaster.' He kept hopping on his left foot and accidently stood on a stone.

'Ouch!' he yelled and grabbed his foot.

'Thanks for the tip,' Marcus said, walking off toward the Centre. He was clearly annoyed at the pressure that EP was putting on them. Yes, they knew just what it all meant for Hanuama Bay and its environment if they didn't solve it soon, but they knew they could if given a bit more time. Looking down at the beach, he spotted Wally Brecon lying on a towel. Buying a cherry shaved ice for himself and a watermelon one for Megan, he said, 'Meet you back at Parry's in a couple of hours.' He sucked on his ice, 'Mmm, Lio is right,' he said. 'They are so ono.' He smiled, hopping on one foot to imitate Lio and then wandered down on to the beach.

Megan opened the door and went back into the Centre. Alanna was having a hand wrestle with a tourist and there was quite a cheering crowd gathered around. It was an even contest with both of them locked into a huge battle, their faces close with noses almost touching. Alanna's big muscled arm pushed hard and with two more attempts, she flattened her opponent's hand down, in victory. The small crowd cheered and Alanna raised her arms in triumph.

'So that's how the Uma in Hanauma Bay came about,' she said. 'It means hand wrestle. After Kamehameha conquered Oahu in 1795, his wife, Queen Ka'ahumanu came to visit. All sorts of hula dancers and hand-wrestlers came to entertain her and even women joined in, too. That's why it is called 'Hana – for happy women and – uma'. The crowd thanked her for her entertainment and began to wander away. Megan approached her whilst she stood alone, tidying up the wrestling table.

'What can I do for you, young Megan?' she said. 'Did you check out that trail?'

Megan decided that she could trust Alanna, just as Lio had said. 'Alanna, I need your help,' she said. 'I am working with Lio. You know Lio right?'

Alanna raised an eyebrow and a warm smile crept across her face. 'Everyone knows Lio,' she said. 'He is one cute Kama'aina and some sort of detective I think – but he never says much to me. Anyway, what's this all about?'

Megan leant in closer so no one heard. 'Yes, he's a kind of detective if you like and we are trying to figure out who is doing all this dumping of rubbish on one of the most beautiful beaches in the world. You've got to tell me what you know. For starters, who is Travis Taylor – the guy that was earlier on the tour? I thought you knew him. We have reason to believe that he may be involved in this crime. How do you know him? And I think you led me up to Koko Head Loop trail, so I might find something – well I did – and it was more than a blow-your-mind view of the beach, I can tell you. We don't have much time to solve this case before the entire bay is covered in rubbish. Is there somewhere private we can go to talk?'

Alanna was shifting her gaze around the room, all the time Megan was talking. 'Yeah – ya right. I reckon I do know what's going on around here. Someone has got a real problem with how beautiful this place is and that Travis is a trouble-maker, a prankster – but I don't think he's stupid enough to be doing all this. He's been here before visiting his Gran, Sue Taylor – I know that 'cause she runs the recycling centre down the road. She's been running it for years. Her trucks keep coming here to clean up all this mess for us,' she said. 'Ya see that room to the right of the ladies lavatory?' Megan nodded. 'Well, ya go right in there,' she almost whispered, 'and I will come in a couple of minutes and we can talk some more in private. Turn the light on, as it's a dark storage room.'

Megan slowly skirted the walls of the entire room until she reached the door to the storage room. Sneaking a look over her shoulder, she knew no one was looking and so she let herself inside and closed the door behind her. The room was dark. Feeling the wall for the light switch, she jerked her hand away and let out a cry. A hand was on the switch already and it wasn't hers. The next thing she knew, she was being blindfolded and pushed out through a side door.

'Get in,' the voice said. Megan was pushed into a van. It stank. She recognised the voice and the grotty smell. It was Travis.

Chapter Eleven

Wally was lying on his towel and sifting the sand through his fingers. His thoughts seemed a million miles away, when Marcus arrived eating his ice.

'Hiya, Wally,' Marcus said. Wally looked at him as if trying to recall whether he knew the tall blonde lanky boy standing in front of him who was blocking out the hot afternoon sun.

'I'm Marcus. We met on the tour inside the Centre earlier today.'

Wally rubbed the sand with his hand and made a flat surface and drew some stick figures in it. 'Oh, right,' he said. 'Having a nice time are you, Marcus?'

Marcus thought he'd take the plunge and ask questions, given the pressure from EP to solve the case. 'I think you know something about all of this rubbish being dumped in the Bay and the Centre and the threats written in the sand.'

Wally stopped drawing in the sand and looked up. His grey beard was long and he stroked it with deep consideration.

'You do?' he said and then remained silent.

Marcus waited for Wally to speak up. When he didn't Marcus told him more about his quest to find out who was destroying the beach.

'I am an historian, Marcus,' he said. 'I am interested in this Bay and how it has changed over the years and the people who come here – how their behaviour has had to change too.' He stood up and shook out his towel before slinging it around his neck.

'Why don't you come with me for a walk and I'll show you how spectacular the view is from up above.'

They slowly walked the same path as Megan had earlier in the day. Almost reaching the peak, Wally stepped off the path on to the reserve.

'Come over this way and you'll get an even better view,' he said.

Wally parted the dense shrubs and Marcus saw the Bay as a huge turquoise bowl of water below. It was edged with white sand and palm trees. He turned his head toward the other direction and was horrified. It was just as Megan had described it – mounds of rubbish piled high like ant-hills dotting the ground, but so much bigger.

'It's beautiful, isn't it?' Wally said, staring at the rubbish piles. 'A wonderful contrast to the beauty of the Bay, don't you think?'

Marcus spun his head from the rubbish to Wally. 'So you know about all this?' he shouted. 'YOU are behind this hideous environmental crime!'

Wally crossed his arms and smiled. 'I wouldn't look at it that way. It's more of a scientific experiment if you like. You see, I am trying to see how the environment is altered by it and whether it really would change the way people feel about the place – will they stay loyal to it once it has withered and died away? Will they still be drawn to the place that was once so beautiful, but now is tainted with mankind's own existence – with rubbish?'

He ushered Marcus to walk toward the mounds of rubbish. Marcus could see the cauldron bubbling over with the gluey substance that Megan had earlier described. Why Parry had not been able to locate this headquarters of the crime was ridiculous – it should have been visible to the naked eye from down on the beach. Yet Marcus couldn't remember seeing anything unusual when he had looked up here.

'You're wondering why you didn't see it before from down below, aren't you?' Wally asked. 'Rather an ingenious little experiment of mine too – I have an invisible force-field surrounding the plant. You can't see it with the naked eye or infra-red laser either. It's as if it doesn't even exist. You see, Marcus, I was a scientist before I turned to history.'

Marcus shook his head at the mad historian-scientist, for that was surely what he must be, for doing all of this. Standing amongst piles of stinking rubbish that was glued together felt like being on some wasteland planet that grew mountains of nothing good. It was useless, meaningless litter destined to lie in the ground and water for years and years before it decayed and became one with the environment. It was plain evil to think Wally could do his experiment in a place so beautiful.

'What's the matter, Marcus?' Wally asked in a slow steady voice. 'You seem a little confused by all of this, poor boy.'

Marcus' gaze burned into Wally's vacant-looking face. 'Confused? No, I'm not the one confused here. But tell me this, why did you think it necessary to choose Hanauma Bay, when you could have chosen any other place to destroy if you had it in your crazy brain to do so? And secondly, why did you think it necessary to bring me here, especially when you knew I would go back and report you immediately.'

It was then that Wally let out his loudest, most awful bellowing laugh yet. The sound made Marcus realise just how mad the grey-haired bearded man was, standing before him with his arms open wide like some worshipper of evil.

'Oh, you are so very innocent, poor boy,' he said, patting Marcus' shoulder. 'Hanauma Bay has been a special place to me for many years. In answer to your

70

second question, well – you're not going anywhere. You are my visitor now. While you may have paid an entrance fee down on Hanauma Bay, you'll be paying an exit fee if you want to leave here alive!' He kept on laughing like a madman.

Marcus began trying to decide which way was best to run for his life but, as he turned he ran straight into the chest of none other than Travis Taylor. Travis placed both hands heavily down on Marcus' shoulders. They seemed to weigh as much as the rocks jutting out of the grassy cliffs. Travis led him around the corner to a hidden caravan.

'Now this time you are not getting away,' he said.

Chapter Twelve

Travis shoved Marcus hard causing him to fall on to the floor inside the caravan. The door was slammed shut and bolted. There was some sand on the floor and from where Marcus was lying face down, he could just make out from the corner of his eye, a girl's foot in a pink flip-flop.

'Megan! What are you doing here?' He jumped up and untied the blindfold and mouth gag so she could speak. She shook her hair free and wiped the dryness from the sides of her mouth.

'Thanks, Marcs. I could say the same for you, but looks like while we've been watching others, others have been watching us.' She parted the grotty mustard and ketchup stained curtains, but it was impossible to see anything through the equally filthy glass windows. Inside the caravan it was far from cosy and inviting – the bed sagged in the corner as if the mattress had long ago given up all hope of comfort. The cupboards were full of rubbish and rotten food.   Mould grew like green furry creatures in the corners of the drawers.

'Charming place,' Megan said. 'No one could possibly sleep in here.   It's disgusting.'

Marcus clapped his hands together as if solving a problem he'd been thinking about.

'That's precisely the point, Megs,' he said. 'This is what it is meant to be – a filthy place.   Don't you see what he's trying to do?'

Megan stood up from the grimy sofa that she had felt herself sticking to, and patted her legs as if to clean them.

'Wally wants this place so filthy and littered that no one will ever want to come here. That's why he's infesting the beach, the Education Centre and the Bay with rubbish. He's even turned this caravan into a tip in case others stumble upon it. It is as if he wants it all for himself.'

Megan paced up and down the small dirty space. 'Okay, but he's destroying the place. There will be nothing left to enjoy – not even for him. I mean look at this caravan – how can he live in it?'

She opened a cupboard door at the side, near the door. The door closed shut before she could glimpse inside, so she opened it again, but quickly shut it when she saw yet more rubbish. Megan gasped – somehow the opening and shutting of the door twice had activated a secret panel to open at the rear of the caravan.

'Wow! What have we got here?' Marcus said, slowly walking toward it. A passageway carved out of rock was now right in front of both of them.

'Megs! That's why the van is wedged so close to the rock face – I bet it's concealing a secret passageway to exactly where Wally truly lives. Come on! Let's see where it goes.'

'Wait, Marcus,' Megan said. 'We should let Parry know what's going on – text him on the iPhone.'

Marcus looked blank. 'Ah – problem there,' he said. 'I forgot my bag and left it inside Parry.' Megan rolled her eyes – it wasn't the first time Marcus had forgotten his devices when they were so needed.

'Okay,' she sighed. 'We'll use our helmets for torch-lights – after you.'

They rubbed the peaks of their caps and transformed them into helmets. Marcus led them down the dark rocky passageway. Megan shivered as she touched the cold jagged walls and the air became colder. Not watching his next step, Marcus stubbed his big toe on a small rock jutting out of the dirt ground. A small trickle of blood oozed into his flip-flop. He wiped it away with the cuff of his sleeve and kept walking to catch up with his sister.

'Take a look at this!' Megan said. They had arrived inside a large room, lit with flame torches mounted to the walls. Tapping the crown of their helmets, they reverted back to ordinary peaked caps.

'We must be inside the centre of the cliff. It's like some sort of cave.' They both looked around at the equipment and Wally's things.

'Cave…?' Marcus said. 'It is more like weird – I mean look at this place. It's like a museum on one side and a factory on the other.' Wally had a sofa, a bed and a camp fire on one side of the cave; on the other was what looked like a massive circular slide tower that reached up over thirty feet high and went down a tunnel to someplace else. Back on the bedroom side, photographs were stuck all over the wall – there must have been hundreds. As Marcus walked toward them, he realised the same person was in every one of them.

'Who is she?' he said. A girl, older than a teenager, was smiling in all of them. Her teeth were straight and white and her eyes sparkled a crystal pale blue. Short wavy blonde hair danced on her suntanned shoulders and dressed in a bikini, she waved to the camera. Marcus instantly recognised the beach as Hanauma Bay. He could even see snorkellers in the shallow water just behind her.

'These photos must be at least thirty years old,' he said. 'I can see the additional car parking lot hadn't been built and the cars are just parked wherever they chose – Alanna mentioned that on the tour.' He kept scanning the photos. Finally, he found one with Wally and the woman in it together. They had arms around each other and looked like girlfriend and boyfriend. His beard was blond and he looked more muscled than how he looked when Marcus met him on the beach. It was more than that though, Marcus thought. Unblinking at the photo, he studied it closely. There was a really happy Wally staring back at him – a happiness he couldn't imagine Wally having now.

Megan was standing well back from Marcus staring at the space above the photos. Her mouth dropped open and her gaze froze. 'Ah, Marcs – look up,' she said.

He stood back and together they stood staring up at a woman's name that had been made out of used rubbish. It said: 'Susannah.' Clumps of rubbish had been carefully glued together to form each of the letters.

'So my guess,' Marcus said, 'is that woman in the photos is…'

'Is Susannah,' a voice said from

behind them. It was Wally and Travis standing to the right of him. They both stood holding shovels. Marcus noticed how Wally stood to attention in front of the shrine-like photo wall.

'You've got something really special here, haven't you, Wally?' Marcus said. 'Is it all for her – the wonderful Susannah?'

'Silence!' yelled Wally. 'How dare you speak her name? She is my reason for it all – and until I make Hanauma Bay die with my rubbish – I will not rest. Go, Travis – tie these children up and prepare the slide for the morning. They can have the pleasure of riding down it at dawn.'

Wally peeled off one of the photos and put it in his pocket. Before leaving them in the hands of Travis, he turned to them both.

'Enjoy it, won't you?' he said. 'It will be the ride to end your lives.'

Chapter Thirteen

Megan kicked and punched Travis as he tied her down on to a board. He strapped green rope around her at least ten times, until she couldn't move her arms or legs. He had hung Marcus on a hook on the cave wall.

'You won't get away with this, Travis!' Marcus yelled. 'If you think this is some kind of stupid prank you like to play on others, you are more of an idiot than I already think you are.'

Travis chuckled. He pulled out an uneaten hamburger from his grubby shorts pocket and devoured it in one mouthful. Stuffing the used wrapper into Marcus' mouth, he burped hamburger breath into his face and tied his hands and feet together. Marcus could feel the back of his white long shirt beginning to tear from the weight of being hung on the hook.

'I'm not an idiot,' Travis said. 'I'm just putting out the rubbish like a good lad.' He cupped his hand around Marcus' chin, squeezed it until it hurt and left the cave laughing.

Megan and Marcus were left alone in the flame torch-lit cavernous room. The board that Megan was tied to was sitting on the slide, which looked like a gigantic sausage of sticky rubbish compressed behind her – ready to go down the slide to the beach. She struggled to free her hands, but it was no good. She was bound so tight to the board that she couldn't free herself. Every time Marcus tried to take his tied hands to the side-seam of his swimming trunks to retrieve his pocket knife, it caused him to swing like the hand on a grandfather clock. Tick-tock, tick-tock – he swung back and forth on the hook, helplessly no closer to freeing himself. As he swayed, time passed silently – but it must have been the entire night. Exhausted from trying to escape, Marcus fell asleep and Megan too, had drifted off. It would only be a matter of a couple of hours before the tower slide was switched on and Megan would be crushed to death amongst the rubbish and spat out onto the beach.

Marcus woke to the sound of the tower slide being switched on. The rubbish was beginning to slowly merge and shift itself. As Marcus tried to scream to wake Megan, he gave a giant sneeze. It was just what was needed to dislodge the wrapper from his mouth.

'Megan!' he shouted. 'Wake up! Wake up!'

Megan stirred and moved her head from side to side to let him know she was awake.

All his shouting made Marcus begin swinging again on the hook and suddenly he realised that if he could swing further he might be able to tear his shirt off completely and fall to the ground. After five attempts, his shirt gave way and he fell to the rock floor to the sound of one great tear. Hands and feet still tied, he hopped over toward Megan. Reaching up to shoulder height he managed to get the gag out of her mouth. He pulled at the ropes that were binding her and was able to loosen them enough for her to get an arm out. Quickly, she unzipped her swimming suit pocket and grabbing her knife, she cut the ropes from her legs.

'Good work, Marcs,' she said. 'Now I have a plan that I think will work. The quickest way out of here is down this slide. There are some old hessian bags hanging on that wall over there – I've been staring at them most of the night. I'll untie you, but be quick – that rubbish is starting to make its slow move. Wally and Travis might come back in here any minute.' Working fast, she cut the ties around Marcus' hands and then he took the knife and freed his own feet. Running over to the wall, he grabbed the bags and swung himself up on to the slide behind Megan.

'Okay, Megs,' he said. 'I've no idea how fast and steep the slide is, but let's get our helmets on and go!'

Rubbing the peaks on their caps, they transformed them into the hi-tech helmets. Pressing the button on the opposite side to the laser ray gun activated a torch to come on at the top of the helmet. Visors down to protect their faces, they climbed into their hessian

82

bags and pushed off before the rubbish almost touched Marcus' shoulders. At first it reminded Marcus of the tall slides at Black Gang Chime Park they once visited on the Isle of Wight – it was bumpy and fast with the air gusting around. But soon enough, this became faster than any slide they had ever been on. The tunnel turned and swerved and was jet-black except for their helmet torch lights. Their vision was jumpy and blurred and their bodies were travelling down such a steep decline that they almost flew than slid. Then all of a sudden it began to flatten out a little and they were lying more horizontal rather than vertical. Megan tilted her head up and could make out a light at the end of the tunnel. It was not just any light – it was the light of the morning sun. As she realised this, she shot out of the tunnel at what felt like rocket speed and rolled on to the sands of Hanauma Bay. Marcus landed about two feet behind her. Whilst they were expecting a speedy landing, they were not expecting to be on film – right in front of them was none other than

Hilary McRoy with her camera on a tripod, filming their spectacular arrival.

'And cut!' she said to herself. 'Well! Good morning to you both – that was rather a surprise, wouldn't you say, for both of us? Just what exactly are you doing and what are those astronaut-like helmets that you are both wearing? And that slide is amazing – funny I never saw it before on the beach. Does it just come out on Tuesdays? I've been filming it for my documentary this past hour.'

'Tuesday!' exclaimed Megan. 'The beach is closed.' She turned to Marcus. 'Wally's doing it today, so no one will be here to see the destruction.' She turned to Hilary. 'Mrs McRoy,' she said, 'you have got to leave the beach. There's no time to explain – but you have to leave the area. The beach is closed as you know on Tuesdays, but it is especially dangerous right now.'

Megan and Marcus didn't wait to explain themselves any further and began to run up the beach. Hilary was left there calling out to them and wanting to know what was going on as she packed her film gear. There was no time to waste. They had to get back to Parry.

Chapter Fourteen

'I am pleased that you are both okay,' Parry said, as soon as they entered the beach hut. 'I have been scanning the area all night, following Lio's notification that you were missing.'

'Lio…?' Marcus asked, reaching for another long sleeve top from the shelf.

'Yes,' Parry said. 'Alanna contacted him when Megan had gone missing from the storage room. She suspected something had happened to you. When you didn't appear either, Marcus, we knew you were both in danger. I have managed to track Travis' accomplice, Marcus – the one collecting the rubbish and who threw you into the van – and I've learnt more about Sue Taylor, his grandmother – but for now please explain everything that has been going on. I have breakfast cereal bars and fruit juice for you, in the cupboard beneath me.'

'Oh, thanks, Parry,' Megan said, reaching for the cupboard and handing out the breakfast. 'We have barely any time. The beach is about to be completely spewed on by rubbish if we don't get down there. We'll explain everything as you transport us there now.'

They sat in the candy-striped deck chairs and placed the boat garland that was strung on white-washed twine across their laps. It transformed into their highly secure seat belts. They rubbed their peaked caps to transform them once again into the hi-tech helmets. Within seconds, Parry whisked them off to the beach – giving Megan long enough to explain the events to Parry and for Marcus to text Lio from his iPhone, which he had found in his bag that was left on the chair.

As they landed, Parry was careful to keep the invisibility shield on, so no one could see them. Megan pressed the rope knot on one side of the lifebuoy, releasing the control panel, which gave them a clear view of the end of the bay where the tunnel slide was still positioned. Parry stood straight in front of it about twenty feet away. Hilary McRoy was now sitting at the side of the beach with her camera, cleaning some of the equipment. Hopefully, she would remain distracted with her head down, a little while longer.

'Look!' Marcus said, pointing to the side of the control panel screen. 'It's Wally and Travis. They are walking down the trail. They must be coming down from the cave to watch it all spew out on to the beach.'

'That won't be happening, Marcus,' Parry said. 'My scanner can detect the rubbish about to enter the beach within fifteen seconds. At that precise point, I will block its entry and cause a gale force-field one hundred times stronger than a winter's storm on Bexhill seaside, to push the litter back up into the cave.'

Parry commenced countdown, 'Ten, nine, eight, seven…'

'Ah, Parry?' Marcus asked. 'Don't you think that's a bit too strong – it may cause a volcanic eruption?'

Parry continued the countdown. 'Possibly, Marcus, but my laser rays will evaporate any trace of rubbish or explosion. Six, five, four…'

'Parry, stop!' screamed Megan. 'Wally and Travis are standing right near the entrance to the tunnel – if you aim now, they will be in the way.'

Marcus charged out of the beach hut, making sure Hilary was not looking up and Wally and Travis were staring into the mouth of the tunnel.

'Get out of the way! You will be harmed if you don't!'

As soon as they saw Marcus, they began to run after him along the beach. Marcus stumbled in the sand, but kept his distance from Parry's aim and managed to get the others out of the way.

'Three, two, one,' Parry counted. 'Fire…!'

What looked like a decorative chimney stack on the roof of the beach hut began to curve and point toward the mouth of the slide tunnel. It released an almost deafening sound of wind that blew directly into the mouth of the slide. As the first sight of gooey rubbish and gunk almost touched the sand, the force of the wind sent it reeling like a hurricane back inside and up the tunnel. Marcus stopped running at the sound and covered his ears. Wally and Travis did the same. They had no idea where the wind that was aimed at the tunnel slide was coming from, as they could not see Parry. Hilary was at a distance and filming it all on camera.

The hurricane sound moaned louder as the rubbish was pushed back up the mountain and into the cave.

'Decreasing pressure,' Parry confirmed. 'Rubbish almost confined.'

Megan studied the control panel screen for levels of stabilisation. Her eyes bulged in shock as she saw signs of rumbling inside the mountain.

'Parry!' she yelled. 'The pressure is too high. The rubbish can't compress any further – it needs to escape. The mountain cannot contain it for much longer – it's going to explode!'

Parry's controls flashed green and amber lights as he adjusted from wind force to directing the laser obliterator.

'Amount of rubbish was more than earlier suspected. Prepare for volcanic eruption of rubbish,' Parry said in his cool and calm voice. 'Three…, two…, one…! Eruption commencing…aiming now.' Almost instantly, the mountain rooftop slit opened and Parry struck the entire eruption with one massive blast – leaving no trace of rubbish anywhere. The soil settled down again, closing the mountain back to normal.

'No!' Wally yelled. 'My masterpiece – it's ruined!' He fell to the ground and buried his face in the sand. His sobbing was all that could be heard. Travis turned to chase Marcus.

'Thanks as ever, Parry,' Megan said, 'but I better get out there.' She quickly closed the door to the beach hut and appeared on the beach at the same time as Lio, Alanna and the police. Travis was captured and thrown down on to the sand by Lio; a police officer hand-cuffed him behind his back. They cuffed Wally who was still sobbing in the sand nearby. Hilary McRoy kept on filming it all, as they were led away to the police van.

Hanauma Bay was safe once again.

Chapter Fifteen

Lio gently patted his big hand on both Marcus and Megan.

'You did well; real well,' he said. 'EP is highly impressed with your success in this mission. But they want to know why Wally Brecon and Travis Taylor were so bent on destroying Hanauma Bay.'

Alanna stood by smiling at Lio talking. Megan noticed how her round cheeks were blushing and she kept smoothing her dark frizzy hair.

'Wally told us that he was doing an experiment to see if people would still come here if it was littered and polluted,' Marcus began.

'But that was really only half the reason he did this,' Megan said. 'Of course no one would want to keep coming to a polluted Hanauma Bay. His real reason was the obsessive love he had for Susannah – a woman who many years ago didn't love him back.'

'Susannah?' Lio said. 'Who's this babe? I'd like to meet her.'

Megan passed around one of the photos of Susannah she had taken off Wally's cave wall.

Alanna frowned and looked a little annoyed by what Lio had said. 'If ya mean Susannah or Sue Taylor – she is about sixty-five these days and runs the recycling plant down the road. Remember I was telling ya about her? She looks older than she does in this photo but it's her, all right.'

'That's the one,' Megan said. 'She was Wally's girlfriend over thirty years ago, but she didn't want to leave Hawaii and she didn't want to be with Wally any more either.'

'Story has it,' Alanna continued. 'That she was so wanting to help the clean-up and protection of Hanauma Bay, she started up the recycling plant. She has played a big part in keeping Hanauma Bay beautiful.'

Lio was nodding to everything they were saying. Megan noticed him smiling at Alanna.

'So he never got over her,' he said, 'and if he couldn't have her, then he wanted to destroy the very beach that she has cared for all of her life.'

'That's about it,' Megan said. 'Plus he didn't want anyone else ever enjoying this beach. He sort of was the kam 'aina that you mentioned, Alanna – someone upset about the preservation. You're right – he must be mad and incredibly smart to have plotted this crime all out, to build a cave, to invent his own invisibility shield around the site and to use the very rubbish that came from Susannah's recycling plant.'

'And that's where Travis comes in,' Marcus continued. 'Travis is Susannah's grandson and had gotten into the wrong sort of crowd of friends – I was unlucky to have met one of them who threw me into his van just for some kind of joke. Travis had been failing at college and his parents sent him to spend time with his grandmother, to help her out at the plant. He hated her and his parents for making him stay in Hawaii so far away from home. Beaches were never his thing and when he met up with Wally Brecon – well, Wally offered him money to steal the rubbish, plant the rubbish inside the Education Centre, graffitti the wall and beach and be part of his plan to destroy Hanauma Bay.'

Lio shook his head as he took it all in. 'Well, Wally is sure one messed up dude,' he said. 'He never got over her.' He straightened up and shook hands with Megan and Marcus. 'Thanks to you two, another beach is kept safe. Well done and keep in touch.' He turned to Alanna, who was smiling at him. 'I know the beach is closed today, but would you like to take a walk with me?'

Megan and Marcus said their goodbyes and watched them walking down the beach. It wasn't long before they noticed Lio and Alanna holding hands.

'Sure is a beautiful and peaceful beach on Tuesdays,' Marcus said, staring out into the turquoise waters. Just then a high-pitched voice called out to them both and broke the calm. It was Hilary McRoy.

'Could you help me for just a minute?' she said, beneath her visor and camera equipment all draped about her. 'You see, I've been watching the film back and I can't understand how or where that wind came from – it was as if it was on the beach…and then I saw what looked like a laser ray aim up to the mountain, but there was nothing on the beach where it seemed to be coming from…and where did you get those incredible-looking helmets you were wearing earlier – I swear you almost looked like astronauts!' She went on: 'I knew that historian was crazy when I first met him. I argued with him in the car park about helping me lug my camera equipment up the koko trail with me. Well, he wasn't one ounce of a gentleman and told me not to go up there.'

Megan and Marcus grinned and were relieved that was all she had on film. Parry's invisibility shield worked under all situations. They pretended to be as baffled as she was about it all and explained that their helmets were just toys. Now all the action had left and Hanauma Bay was basking in peaceful sunshine without one tourist around,

Hilary McRoy decided her filming session had ended and left.

'Time for us to go too, Megs,' Marcus said. They looked in the direction of where Parry was standing. Then they looked around the curve of the beach. Not one person was there – it was a rare sight.

'Just a quick last snorkel before we go?' Megan said.

Marcus nudged his sister toward Parry. 'Remember, Megs – no swimming on Tuesdays,' he said. 'We also have to abide by the rules.' They entered the beach hut and strapped themselves into their candy-striped deck chairs.

'Thanks again, Parry,' Marcus said. 'Hanauma is clean and safe again. Now it's time for me to clean up, too.' He opened Lio's antiseptic hand gel and rubbed his hands clean.

Megan reached over for it, too. 'I need a bucket of that stuff,' she said. 'I smell horrible.'

'No offence, Megs,' he said. 'But you do really stink!'

Parry's lights flashed a happy shade of

green and they commenced take-off back to Bexhill-on-Sea.

Chapter Sixteen

The landing was smooth and the air was cooler. All devices were returned to their hidden compartments. A banging was heard on the door, so Megan opened it. It was their beach hut neighbour, little Charlotte Cook.

'Oh, hi, Charlotte,' she said. The little girl was holding a big hamper of food and drink that was all wrapped up with a big ribbon on the top. Mr and Mrs Cook came out to stand behind her. Marcus joined Megan and stood in the doorway to Parry.

'Hi, Mr and Mrs Cook. Hi, Charlotte,' he said. 'What's this?'

Charlotte handed it to Megan. 'It is for you,' she said. 'I did what you said.'

Megan looked puzzled.

'About the ring…' Charlotte said. 'I told my mum and dad and we took it to the police. Dad said it wasn't the sort of thing from the beach that I should keep and he was right. The police said there was a one hundred pound reward for anyone who found it on the beach and handed it in.'

Behind her, her parents were smiling. 'This is just a token of our appreciation for helping Charlotte do the right thing,' Mr Cook said.

Megan and Marcus were shocked at the kindness – especially the honesty shown by Mr Cook. They didn't think he would have been so willing to hand in the ring.

'You are welcome,' Megan said. 'You didn't have to give us this, but we are rather hungry and those pasties smell delicious. So thank you.'

They were about to go back inside the beach hut when Mr Cook raised a finger. 'Perhaps you could be so kind to let us take a look around the back of your beach hut.' He licked his lips. 'There might be some more jewellery that needs finding and monetary rewards given out.'

Mrs Cook poked him in his side and they all laughed. Waving and thanking again they were about to go back to their own beach huts when Mrs Cook said,

'Oh, dear – what's that awful smell? It smells worse than the Pebsham rubbish tip!' Megan and Marcus looked at each other.

'Oh, we've just been doing some cleaning. They smiled and closed Parry's aqua- coloured door behind them.

'Now let's open this hamper up and eat,' Megan said. 'Showering can happen later. I'm starving.'

Parry released a fine fragrance of tropical breeze spray inside the beach hut to help clean the air and spoke up.

'You may wish to also open this up.' The cabinet beneath his voice box opened, revealing a small black velvet jewellery pouch. 'I scanned the area outside behind me and detected it.'

Marcus jumped up and grabbed the bag. Undoing the cord, the pouch loosened in his palm and dozens of diamonds and pearls sprouted up to the top.

'Sick!' Marcus said. 'The ring must belong to all of this.'

Megan came over and stared down at all the treasure. 'Now it's our turn to hand it in to the police. It must be stolen – wow – it has to be worth hundreds of thousands of pounds.'

Marcus nodded. 'But it reminds us of one thing as EP agents, going to all the most exotic beaches in the world.'

'What?' Megan asked.

'Bexhill-on-sea sure is one very special place.'

'Yes,' said Megan. 'As Lio would say – it's so ono!'

They both laughed and settled down to eat pasties.

The End

So maybe you want to go to Hanauma Bay, Hawaii. Here are some facts and legend…

- Legend has it that two warriors fell in love with the same woman. So they hand wrestled each other at Hanauma Bay to decide who would marry her, but she was scared they would hurt themselves wrestling. So she decided to go and turn herself into a beautiful nearby mountain. It is now called Koko Crater. She did this so both men could look up at her forever

- Facts state that Hanauma Bay is about 10 miles from Waikiki Beach in Honolulu on the island of O'ahu in Hawaii

- Hawaii is located in the north central Pacific Ocean and is made up of a string of 137 islands

- Hanauma Bay is a country nature park and a state underwater park with strict rules about how to behave and care for its environment

- Honolulu county spent millions and millions of dollars to build the Hanauma Bay Education Centre

- It is a protected area for young green sea-turtles

- All visitors are expected to watch a video at the education centre and pay an entrance fee to the beach

- Arrive early to the beach to avoid the crowds – only limited numbers of tourists are allowed on the beach each day

- Tuesdays are closed to the general public – that means you, so let the fish swim alone and come back on Wednesday!

- If you forget your snorkels – shame on you! It's one of the best bays in the world to go snorkeling. Don't worry – you can hire gear like snorkels and there are lockers to put your other stuff in while you are out in the bay

- Hanauma Bay has been voted 'Best Beach in USA'

About the Author

Cathy Maisano is a cultural researcher who spends her time learning about different places and people. As a child growing up in Australia, her back gate opened directly on to a beach lined with different coloured beach huts and she spent many happy hours playing among them and choosing her favourite one. Nowadays, having travelled to many beaches around the world on research projects, Cathy has an expert knowledge of their differences and the environmental problems facing so many of them. Currently, she lives almost quite literally right on a beach in Sydney, Australia with her husband and children.

Printed in Poland
by Amazon Fulfillment
Poland Sp. z o.o., Wrocław